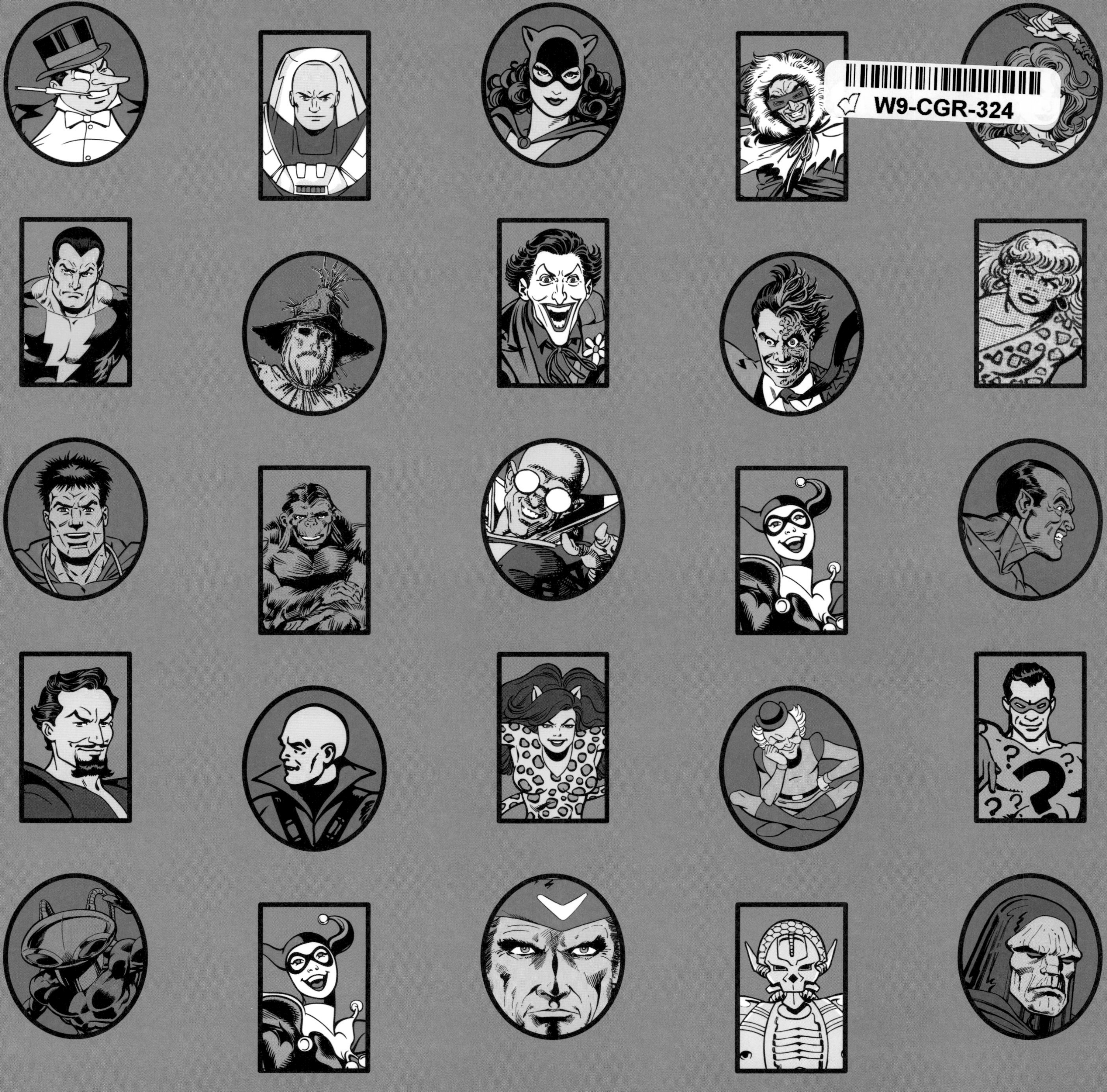

THE BIG BOOK OF
SUPER-VILLAINS

by Morris Katz

downtown bookworks

downtown bookworks

Downtown Bookworks Inc.
265 Canal Street
New York, New York 10013
www.downtownbookworks.com

Designed by Georgia Rucker
Typeset in Geometric and CCHeroSandwich

Printed in China
March 2018

ISBN 978-1-941367-55-1

10 9 8 7 6 5 4 3 2 1

Powerful super heroes like Superman, Batman, and Wonder Woman work hard every day to keep people safe. But there are lots of super-villains working hard to make trouble! Learn about what these scoundrels were like before their lives of crime. Discover their favorite tools and tricks. See who their archenemies are. You definitely won't want to behave like them!

THE JOKER

LOOK OUT, *GOTHAM!*
THE JOKER'S BACK IN TOWN!

The Joker was not always an evil villain. He started out as a petty criminal. Then, during a simple robbery, he fell into a bubbling tub of toxic chemicals. The chemicals turned his hair green and his skin white. His lips became stuck in a permanent smile. This tragic accident and his strange appearance drove the Joker crazy and led him to torment the citizens of Gotham City.

The Joker sometimes teams up with Batman's other enemies, like the Penguin, the Riddler, and Two-

Face. But he doesn't play very nicely with others, so those alliances never last long. His favorite sidekick of all is Harley Quinn. They met during one of the Joker's stays in Arkham Asylum, a hospital for the criminally insane, where Harley was his psychiatrist. Soon after he became her patient, Harley Quinn began to join the Joker on his evil escapades.

Like Batman, the Clown Prince of Crime doesn't have any superpowers. Instead, he has an impressive bag of tricks—a flower in his lapel that sprays water, exploding cigars, and his famous Joker venom, which makes Batman and Robin laugh uncontrollably! These inventive weapons make it really hard for Batman to catch the Joker.

He may look silly with his colorful face and crooked smile, but there is nothing funny about Gotham City's most wicked villain.

THE PENGUIN

Don't let his silly waddling walk or old-fashioned top hat fool you. The Penguin is one dangerous criminal. He's nearly always up to no good. The Penguin has a knack for knowing what everyone in Gotham City is doing. And he uses that knowledge to make people do what he wants. He strikes fear into the hearts of citizens and keeps Batman and Robin busy.

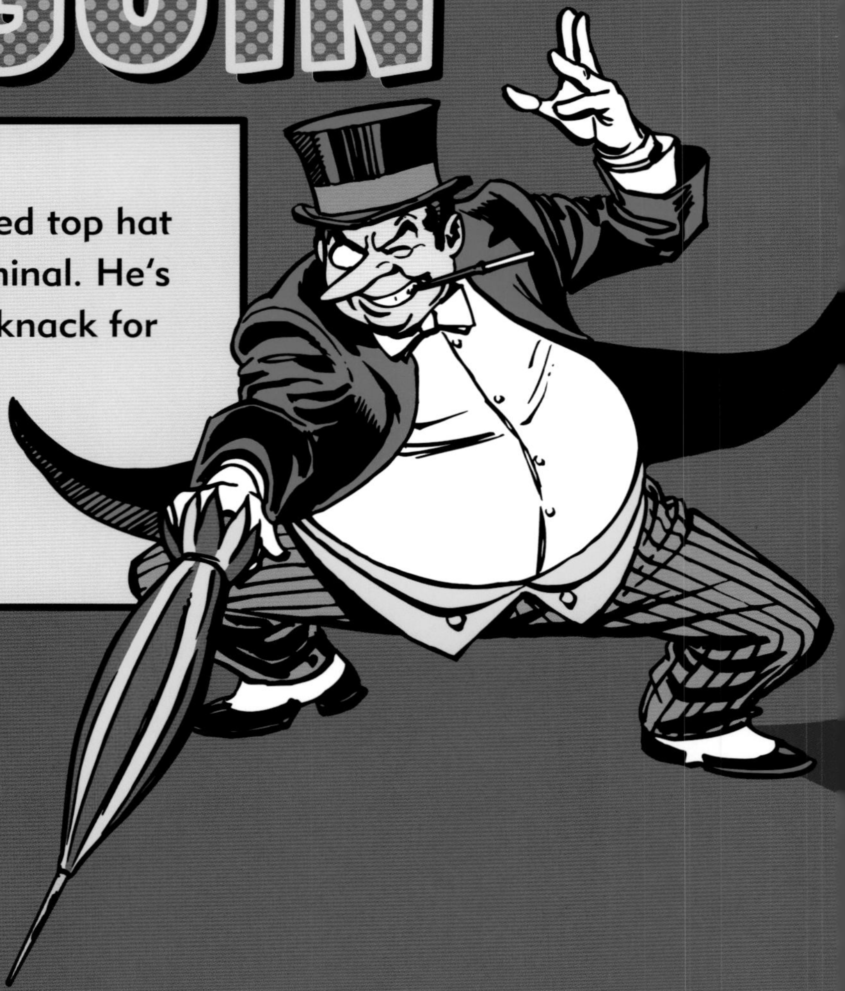

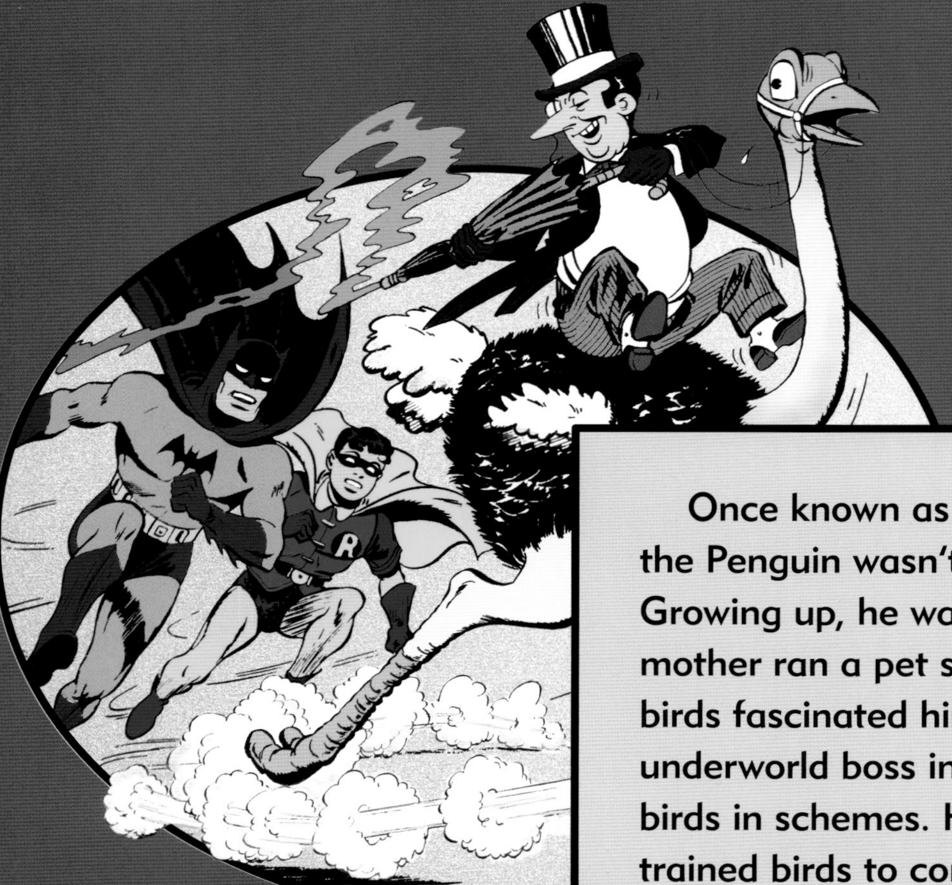

Once known as Oswald Chesterfield Copperpot, the Penguin wasn't always such a troublemaker. Growing up, he was a grumpy little boy whose mother ran a pet shop filled with exotic birds. The birds fascinated him. After the Penguin became an underworld boss in Gotham City, he started using birds in schemes. He's so clever and devious, he even trained birds to commit crimes for him!

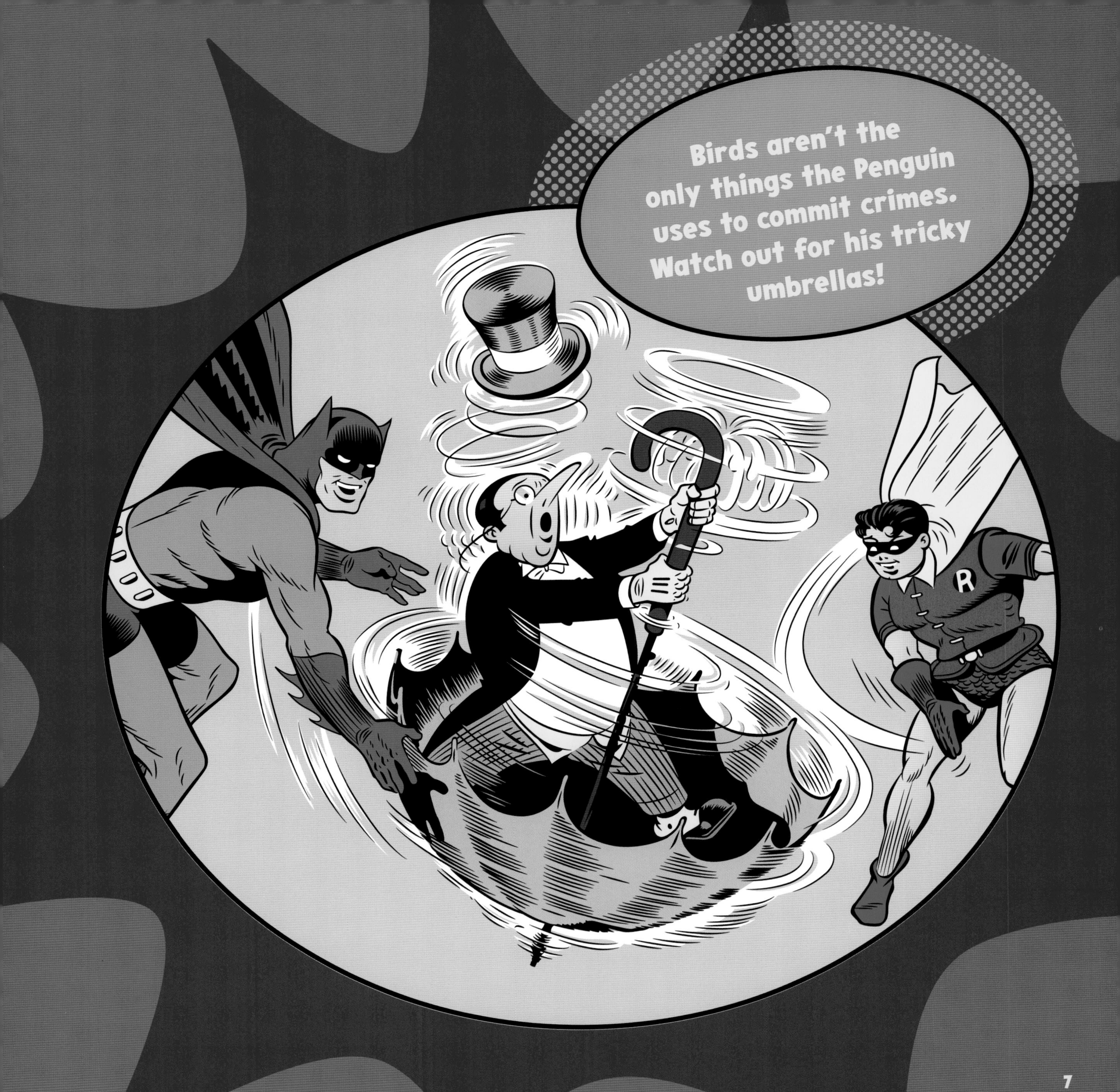
Birds aren't the only things the Penguin uses to commit crimes. Watch out for his tricky umbrellas!

HARLEY QUINN

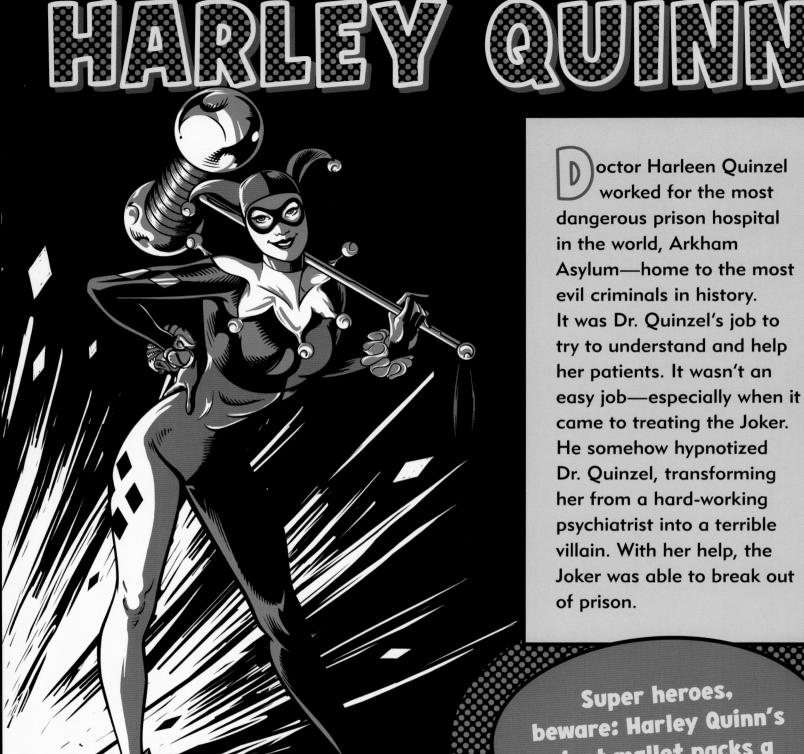

Doctor Harleen Quinzel worked for the most dangerous prison hospital in the world, Arkham Asylum—home to the most evil criminals in history. It was Dr. Quinzel's job to try to understand and help her patients. It wasn't an easy job—especially when it came to treating the Joker. He somehow hypnotized Dr. Quinzel, transforming her from a hard-working psychiatrist into a terrible villain. With her help, the Joker was able to break out of prison.

Super heroes, beware: Harley Quinn's giant mallet packs a mighty punch!

In her life of crime, the not-so-good doctor goes by Harley Quinn. She uses her charm and everything she learned about the human mind to trick people into giving her exactly what she wants. Though she started off as the Joker's sidekick, Harley became a powerful villain in her own right. An enemy of Batman's and really anyone who crosses her, Harley Quinn belongs inside Arkham Asylum as a criminal now.

POISON IVY

amela Isley was a shy and brilliant plant scientist when a risky experiment gave her the ability to control plants. She can trap someone with creeping vines and unleash toxins that allow her to control people's minds.

Poison Ivy battles Batman and Robin, but she saves her most serious schemes for people who hurt the environment. Even though she's a villain, she's not all bad.

Just like the plants she loves, Poison Ivy needs sunlight to survive.

SCARECROW

As a child, Jonathan Crane lived in fear. He hated feeling anxious and set out to conquer his fears. He studied psychology and learned everything he could about what scares people. But he did not use this knowledge to make himself a better person or to help others. Instead, Scarecrow invented a fear toxin that makes people live out their worst nightmares. This cruel criminal is happiest when he is terrifying the citizens of Gotham City.

Scarecrow's creepy mask protects him from his own fear gas.

TWO-FACE

Harvey Dent was once one of Gotham's finest, a district attorney working to convict criminals and clean up the streets. He was even a good friend of Bruce Wayne's. During a trial, he was attacked by a criminal, leaving him with a scarred face and a warped mind.

His name, Two-Face, has several meanings. First, half of his face is normal, and the other half is disfigured. He also makes decisions by flipping a coin—a two-headed silver dollar that is his good-luck charm. And he has two personalities: the original good guy (Harvey Dent) and the villain he has become.

Two-Face even wears two-colored suits made of two different fabrics!

THE RIDDLER

When Batman arrives at the scene of a crime and finds a clue in the form of a riddle, puzzle, or word game, he knows he's dealing with the Riddler.

Edward Nigma was always obsessed with puzzles. For a time, he ran a carnival booth in which people would pay to compete against him in solving a puzzle. But Nigma would rig the puzzles so he won every time. Eventually, the Riddler moved beyond cheating and on to more serious crimes. And he always leaves a riddle for Batman and Robin to solve—just to keep things interesting.

Batman and Robin definitely have to keep their wits about them when they're dealing with the Riddler.

The Riddler is the Prince of Puzzlers.

? HOW CAN ONE GET INTO A LOCKED CEMETERY AT NIGHT?

? CAN YOU TELL WHAT NATIONALITY NAPOLEON'S PARENTS WERE?

? WHEN DOES TEN ADDED TO TEN EQUAL TEN?

$$\begin{array}{r} 10 \\ +10 \\ \hline 10 \end{array}$$

? WHY IS THE LETTER "A" LIKE A HONEYSUCKLE?

A

CATWOMAN

Much like her enemy Batman, Selina Kyle was orphaned as a child in Gotham City. But unlike Bruce Wayne, she did not have millionaire parents. Selina had to steal from people in order to survive on her own. Over the years she got better and better at stealing, and she developed a taste for expensive jewelry, especially diamonds. The scale of her crimes grew as her catlike reflexes became sharper.

> Catwoman's gloves and boots have retractable claws that enable her to scale buildings!

ROGUES' GALLERY

UNDERCOVER POLICE AGENTS

A-B-C

A-B-C

D-E-F

D-E-F

G-H-I

G-H-I

14

MR. FREEZE

Dr. Victor Fries started out as a scientist. He was an expert in cryogenics. That means he studied what happens to people and things in extremely cold temperatures. He used his technology to put his wife, Nora, into a deep freeze because she was dying. (He figured that maybe someday there would be a cure for her disease, and he could bring her back to life.)

A terrible accident in his lab released freezing agents that completely changed Victor's body, transforming him into Mr. Freeze. Suddenly, he could only survive when the temperature around him was below freezing. He developed a special suit to keep his body cold at all times. He uses a freeze gun against Batman—and anyone else who gets in his way.

Mr. Freeze has ice in his veins!

BLACK ADAM

Thousands of years ago, Black Adam was chosen by the council of wizards as their leader. They gave him unimaginable magical powers. But the council did not choose wisely.

Instead of using his powers to help the wizards and others, he used his abilities to control them. After a major battle, the wizards were able to imprison Black Adam for many years. Then they appointed a new champion, Shazam!

Now Black Adam is free again and on a mission—to destroy his enemy Shazam!, seize his magical powers, and rule the world.

Black Adam's powers come from the ancient Egyptian gods.

DR. SIVANA

When you picture a "mad scientist," you are probably imagining someone who looks and acts like Dr. Sivana. He's a crazy, ingenious inventor. But he started out as a hardworking scientist whose ideas were ahead of his time.

When his work was rejected, he became angry and bitter and left Earth to live on the planet Venus. (He flew there with his family in a spaceship he invented.) From there, he plotted his revenge against the world. But every time he tried to get even, he was foiled by Shazam! In addition to figuring out Shazam!'s identity (Shazam! is really a boy named Billy Batson), Dr. Sivana nicknamed him the Big Red Cheese.

When Dr. Sivana's plans are thwarted, he says, "Curses! Foiled again!"

GRODD

Grodd is no ordinary gorilla. Not only is he incredibly intelligent, but he can move objects with his mind and even control other people's thoughts.

How did he get these unusual powers? An alien spaceship crashed near his home in Africa, carrying space rocks that changed him forever. With the help of the alien who crashed, Grodd's tribe built the amazing, technologically advanced Gorilla City. Together, the super-smart gorillas lived in peace. . . until Grodd decided he wanted to take over the world. The Flash foiled that plan, and the two have been fighting ever since.

CAPTAIN COLD

Captain Cold is a cold-hearted criminal. Also known as Leonard Snart, he uses a high-tech freeze gun to stop people in their tracks. His favorite pastimes are making trouble in Central City and trying to stop The Fastest Man Alive.

CAPTAIN BOOMERANG

It's lucky The Flash is so fast because he has quite a few enemies! He is also the frequent target of Captain Boomerang's dangerous boomerangs.

When Digger Harkness was a young boy in Australia, he loved to make and play with boomerangs. As he got older, his "toys" became more complicated and, eventually, deadly. Captain Boomerang's flying weapons can start fires or deliver electrical shocks. And they always return right to his hand.

BLACK MANTA

Black Manta was a regular kid who lived on a houseboat. He became a skilled diver, searching the seafloor for gold and other ancient treasures.

He can't breathe underwater like his archenemy Aquaman can. But Black Manta built a high-tech suit that enables him to breathe deep down under the sea and a helmet that blasts energy rays. He also designed a submarine that looks like a manta ray. In it, he can travel great distances, as he chases after Aquaman and even tries to attack Aquaman's homeland, Atlantis.

The seas are not safe when Black Manta is lurking around.

SINESTRO

There are Green Lanterns all over the galaxy. They are strong, creative, and willing to stand up for peace. Green Lanterns get their special powers from their power rings. (They have to keep the rings charged, or they lose their power!)

Sinestro started out as a member of the Green Lantern Corps from the planet Korugar. But, when he got a taste of power, he became selfish. Eventually, he grew so evil he was banned from the Green Lantern Corps.

Sinestro found a new home. And he created the Sinestro Corps of Yellow Lanterns, who use the power from their yellow rings to try to rule the universe. Yellow Lanterns want to be feared—unlike Green Lanterns, who aim to protect people.

Sinestro is the archenemy of Hal Jordan, one of Earth's Green Lanterns.

MY POWER RING IS STUCK TO THE LANTERN-- I CAN'T PULL IT FREE!

YOU'RE BEATEN, GREEN LANTERN! I'VE PROVEN MY POWER RING IS MIGHTIER THAN YOURS!

THE CHEETAH

With her enchanted claws, The Cheetah can cut through almost anything.

Barbara Minerva gets her super-speed and strength from the Plant God Urzkartaga. She also has enhanced senses. She can see, hear, and smell things that regular people can't. She goes by The Cheetah because of her cheetah-like reflexes.

A leader of the Legion of Doom (a group of super-villains that includes Black Manta and Sinestro), The Cheetah has a passion for old, valuable things. She definitely has an eye on Wonder Woman's Golden Lasso— just one of the reasons Wonder Woman is her main rival.

GIGANTA

Giganta is another (rather large) enemy of Wonder Woman. Her real name is Dr. Doris Zeul. Before she became Giganta, Doris had a fatal illness. She used an experimental treatment (involving a gorilla) to cure her disease. The treatment saved her life and gave her the power to grow as big as she wants to be.

Giganta is a *huge* problem for Wonder Woman.

KRAACK!

LEX LUTHOR

One of the most brilliant, sinister super-villains in the world, Lex Luthor is Superman's archenemy. The billionaire head of LexCorp hates Superman not only because he stands in the way of Lex's world domination, but also because he comes from another planet.

Lex is jealous of Superman's powers. He uses his brain and his money to try to defeat Superman—plus, he always keeps some Kryptonite handy in case he needs to weaken Superman.

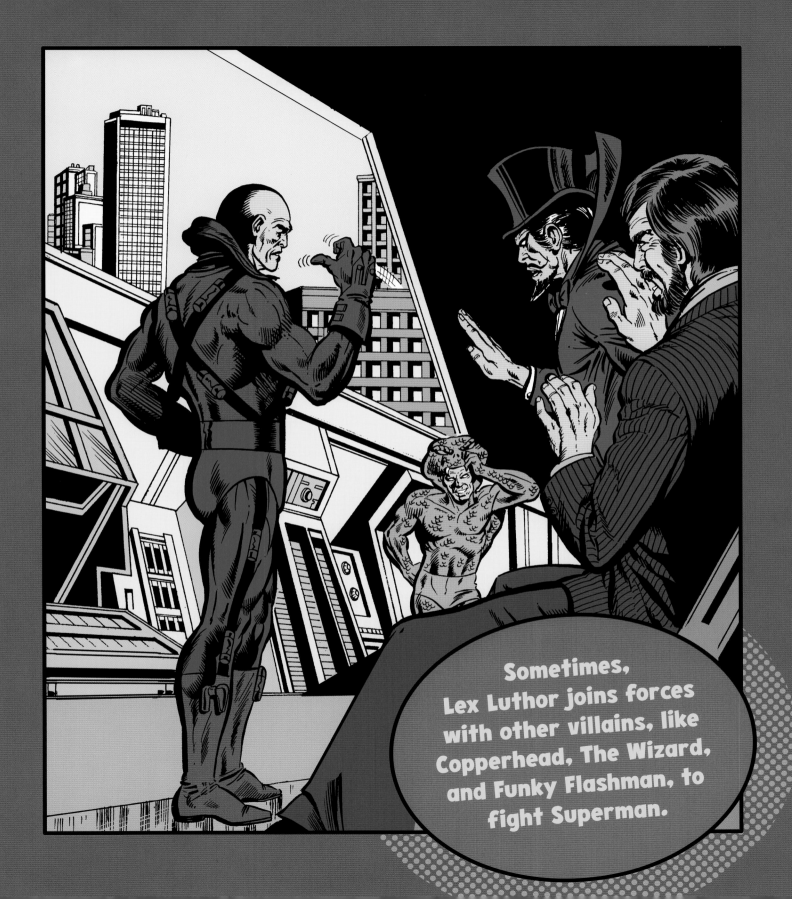

Sometimes, Lex Luthor joins forces with other villains, like Copperhead, The Wizard, and Funky Flashman, to fight Superman.

MR. MXYZPTLK

Mr. Mxyzptlk (pronounced *miks-yez-pittle-ik*) is a magical, troublemaking imp. His power is in his imagination—and his ability to warp reality. He can convince everyone around him that whatever he is imagining is real. He has made Lois Lane forget that she knows Superman! He plays these tricks mostly to entertain himself. His weakness is that if he says his name backward (*kil-tipsy-zim*), he is sent back to his home in the Fifth Dimension. Lucky for Superman, Mr. Mxyzptlk is not very smart and can be easily tricked into reciting his name backward and leaving everyone alone for a while.

Mr. Mxyzptlk loves to play practical jokes—but he gets really angry if anybody pulls a prank on him!

GENERAL ZOD

General Zod was a military leader on the Planet Krypton, Superman's home world. Like Superman, he gets his superpowers from Earth's yellow sun, and he was the son of scientists. That is where their similarities end. Considered a traitor on Krypton, Zod was imprisoned in a place called The Phantom Zone because he tried to start a war. When his prison sentence was up, he took his warlike instincts to Earth. Only Superman is strong enough to defeat Zod.

Even a nuclear blast cannot hurt Zod!

BIZARRO

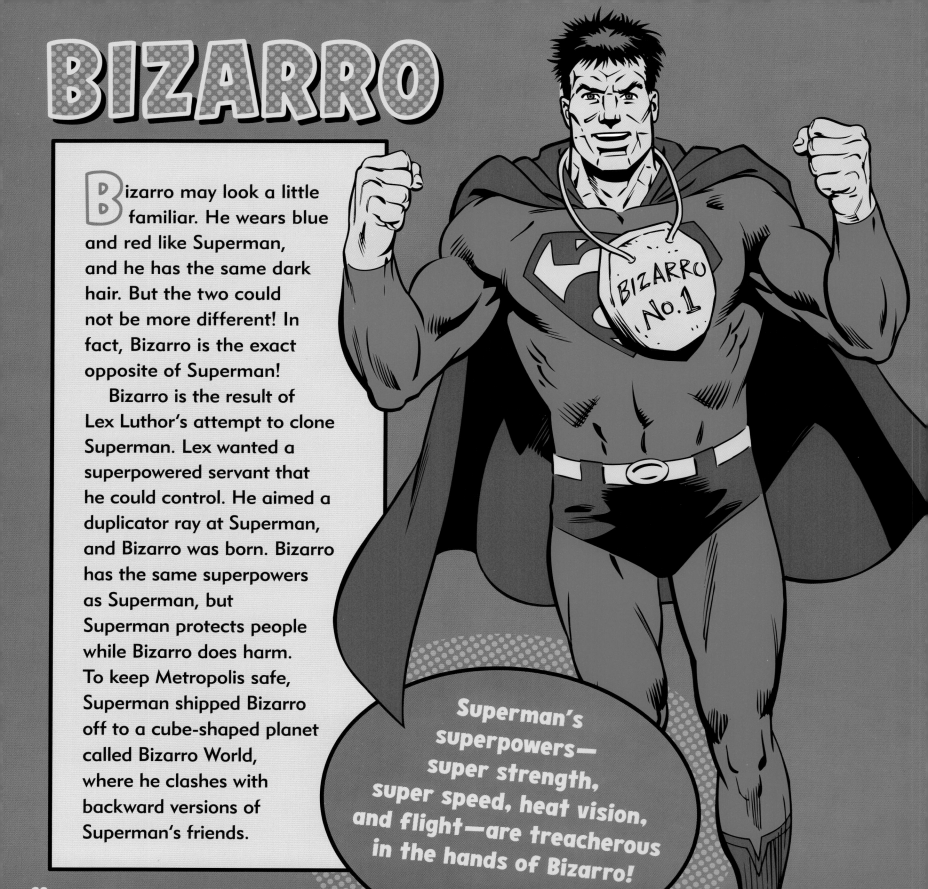

Bizarro may look a little familiar. He wears blue and red like Superman, and he has the same dark hair. But the two could not be more different! In fact, Bizarro is the exact opposite of Superman!

Bizarro is the result of Lex Luthor's attempt to clone Superman. Lex wanted a superpowered servant that he could control. He aimed a duplicator ray at Superman, and Bizarro was born. Bizarro has the same superpowers as Superman, but Superman protects people while Bizarro does harm. To keep Metropolis safe, Superman shipped Bizarro off to a cube-shaped planet called Bizarro World, where he clashes with backward versions of Superman's friends.

Superman's superpowers— super strength, super speed, heat vision, and flight—are treacherous in the hands of Bizarro!

BIZARRO No. 1

BRAINIAC

Brainiac comes from the planet Colu—he is an alien just like Superman. Brainiac also has some serious powers. He is a robot with a computer brain and access to advanced technology. Along with his army of drones, he travels through the universe shrinking cities and entire worlds down to the size of his hand. Then he stores these miniature cities in bottles!

Brainiac's force field belt makes it really hard for Superman to get near him.

With Brainiac, a little technology can be a terrible thing.

DARKSEID

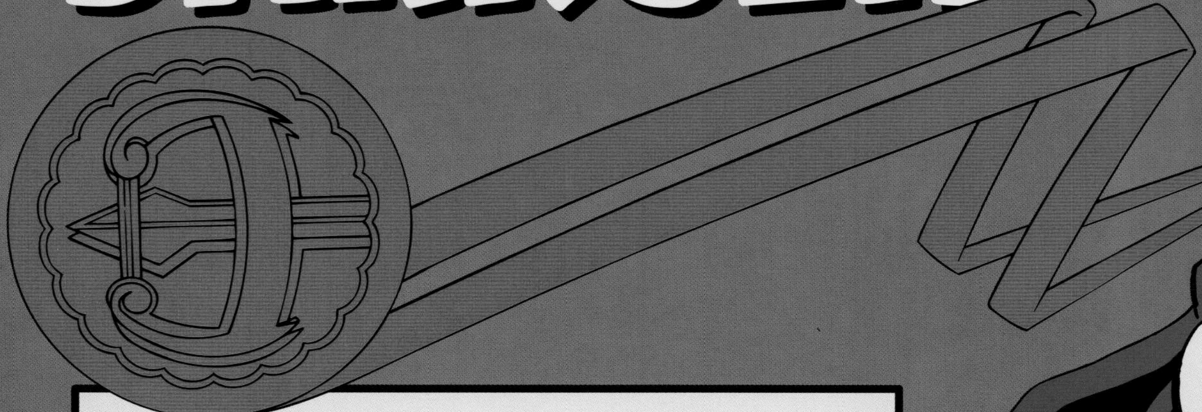

Beware the Omega Beams! Darkseid draws energy from a cosmic power source called the Omega Effect. He can harness this power and focus it into pure energy that he shoots from his eyes. His deadly Omega Beams can destroy anything in their path—or zap people and things to a completely different place in the universe.

Mighty Omega Beams aren't the only tricks Darkseid has. With superhuman speed, superhuman strength, and the ability to read minds and control people's thoughts, he is one of Superman's most powerful enemies.

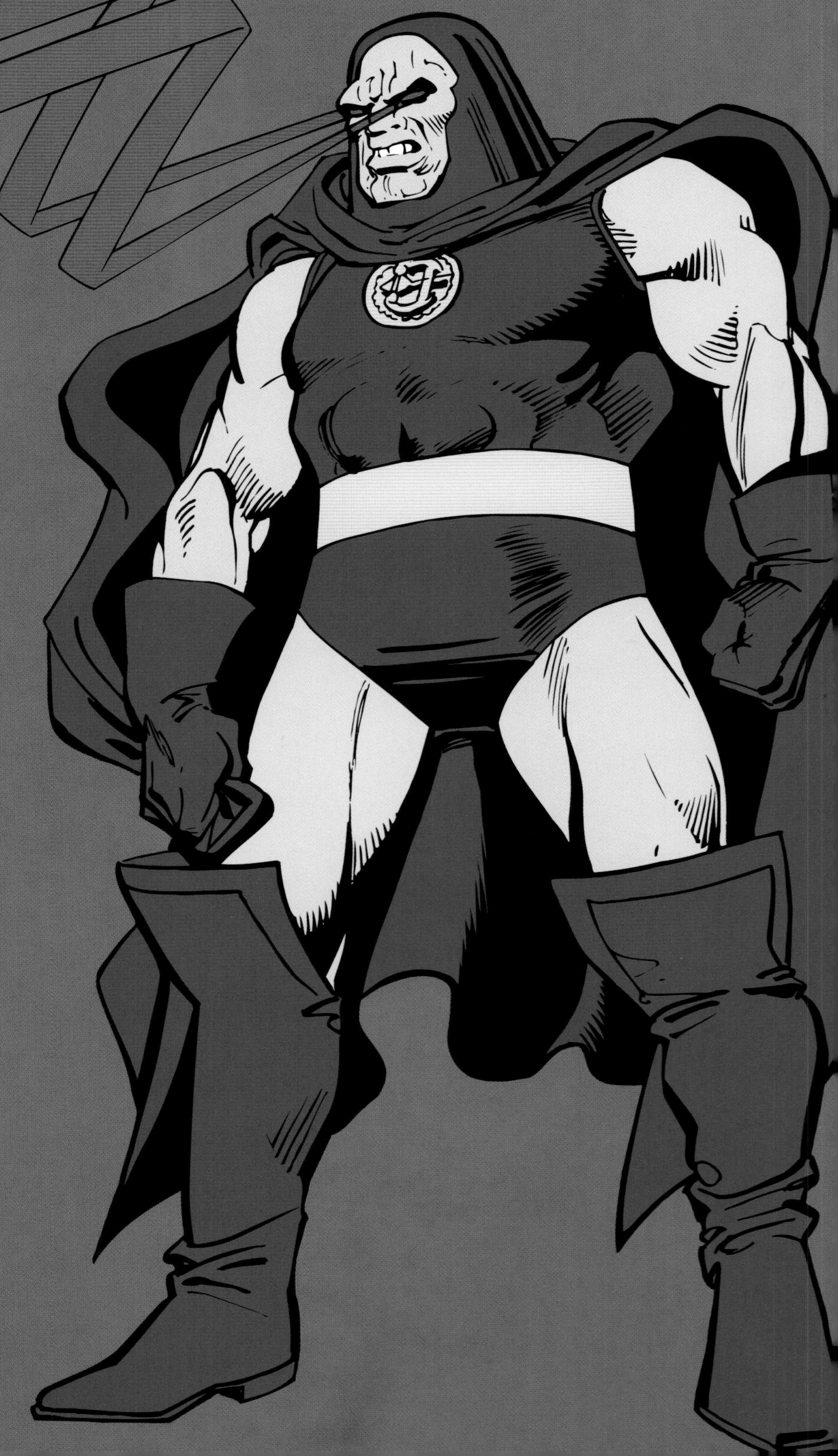

Darkseid rules the planet Apokolips, forcing people to work until they drop. But he wants to control more than just one miserable planet. He wants to take over the entire universe and make every being in it his slave.

Darkseid has an army of flying minions called Parademons. They help him spread terror.

DON'T DO WHAT THEY DO!

These villains have all made bad choices. Instead of using their smarts and skills to help others, they hurt people. Luckily, there are plenty of super heroes—and good people—who fight to make the world a better, safer place.

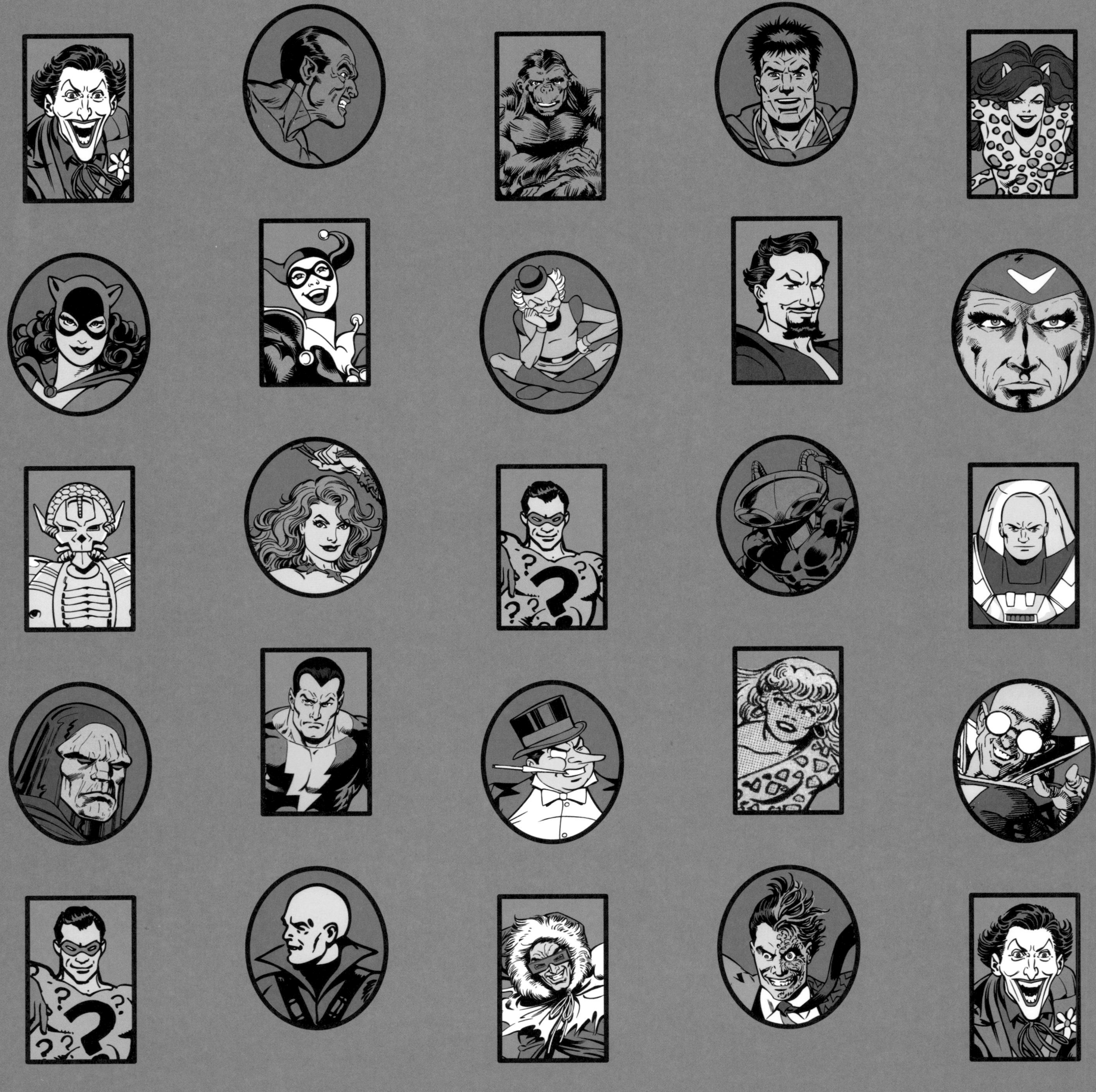